Peanut Butter and Jelly

A PLAY RHYME

illustrated by

NADINE BERNARD WESTCOTT

A TRUMPET CLUB SPECIAL EDITION

to Wendy and Laurie

Published by The Trumpet Club
1540 Broadway, New York, New York 10036

Illustrations copyright © 1987 by Nadine Bernard Westcott

ISBN: 0-440-84477-0

This edition published by arrangement with Dutton
Children's Books, a division of Penguin Books USA Inc.
Designer: Riki Levinson
Printed in the United States of America
October 1991

10 9 8 7 6
UPC

Peanut butter, peanut butter,
Jelly, jelly.

First you take the dough and
Knead it, knead it.

Peanut butter, peanut butter,
Jelly, jelly.

Pop it in the oven and
Bake it, bake it.

Peanut butter, peanut butter,
Jelly, jelly.

Then you take a knife and
Slice it, slice it.

Peanut butter, peanut butter,
Jelly, jelly.

Then you take the peanuts and
Crack them, crack them.

Peanut butter, peanut butter,
Jelly, jelly.

Put them on the floor and
Mash them, mash them.

Peanut butter, peanut butter,
Jelly, jelly.

Then you take a knife and
Spread it, spread it.

Peanut butter, peanut butter,
Jelly, jelly.

Next you take some grapes and
Squash them, squash them.

Peanut butter, peanut butter,
Jelly, jelly.

Glop it on the bread and
Smear it, smear it.

Peanut butter, peanut butter,
Jelly, jelly.

Then you take the sandwich and
Eat it, eat it.

Peanut butter, peanut butter,
Jelly, jelly.

Peanut butter, peanut butter,
Jelly, jelly.

The words in this book are a variation of a popular play rhyme about making a peanut butter and jelly sandwich, from kneading the bread dough, to mashing the peanuts, to finally eating the whole thing.

In between each of the verses below (which include suggested hand and body actions), the rhythmic refrain—with motions—is repeated.

Peanut butter, peanut butter, jelly, jelly.
(clap, slap knees, clap, slap knees clap, slap knees, clap, slap knees)

First you take the dough and knead it, knead it.
(push with heels of hands)——————————— [Refrain]

Pop it in the oven and bake it, bake it.
(extend arm towards "oven")——————— [Refrain]

Then you take a knife and slice it, slice it.
("saw" back and forth with side of hand) [Refrain]

Then you take the peanuts and crack them, crack them.
(pound fists together)——————————————— [Refrain]

Put them on the floor and mash them, mash them.
(push fist into palm of other hand)——————— [Refrain]

Then you take a knife and spread it, spread it.
(move hand back and forth as if spreading) [Refrain]

Next you take some grapes and squash them, squash them.
(stamp feet)————————————————————— [Refrain]

Glop it on the bread and smear it, smear it.
(spreading motion again)——————————— [Refrain]

Then you take the sandwich and eat it, eat it.
(open and close mouth as if biting)————— [Refrain]

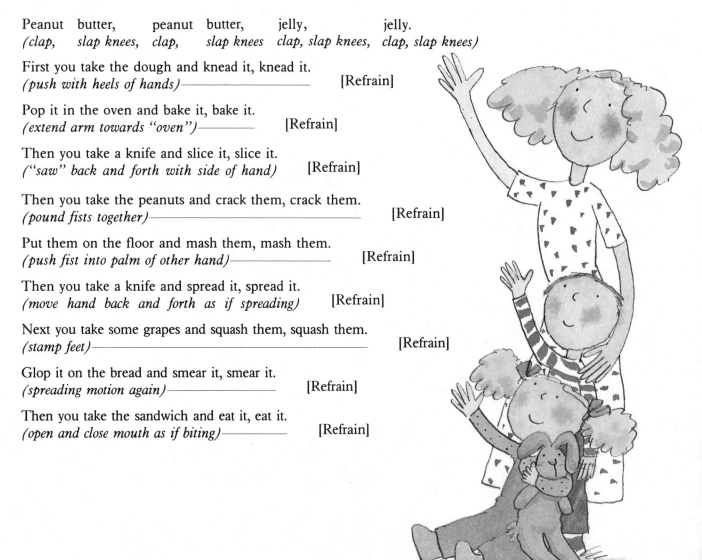